Millie's Marvellous Hat

Also by Satoshi Kitamura:

Angry Arthur
(written by Hiawyn Oram)

Igor, the Bird Who Couldn't Sing

Me and My Cat?

Pablo the Artist

Sheep in Wolves' Clothing

What's Wrong With My Hair?

When Sheep Cannot Sleep

First published in Great Britain in 2009 by Andersen Press Ltd., 20 Vauxhall Bridge Road, London SW1V 2SA.
Published in Australia by Random House Australia Pty., Level 3, 100 Pacific Highway, North Sydney, NSW 2060.
Copyright © Satoshi Kitamura, 2009. The rights of Satoshi Kitamura to be identified as the author and
illustrator of this work have been asserted by him in accordance with the Copyright, Designs and Patents Act, 1988.
All rights reserved.
Colour separated in Switzerland by Photolitho AG, Zürich. Printed and bound in Singapore by Tien Wah Press.

10   9   8   7   6   5   4   3   2   1

British Library Cataloguing in Publication Data available.

ISBN 978 1 84270 924 5

This book has been printed on acid-free paper.

Millie's
Marvellous Hat

Satoshi Kitamura

Andersen Press
London

Millie was walking home from school when she came across a hat shop.
There were lots of hats in the window but the one she liked best was the one with the colourful feathers.

Millie went inside.

"May I see the hat with the colourful feathers, please?"
she asked the man behind the counter.
"Certainly, Madam," replied the man and he fetched the hat
from the window.
Millie tried it on. It suited her perfectly.
"I'll take it," she said.
"An excellent choice, Madam," said the man. "That will be
five hundred and ninety-nine pounds and ninety-nine pence."

Millie opened her purse and looked inside.
"Oh dear," she said. "Do you have anything a little cheaper?"
"What sort of price were you thinking of, Madam?"
asked the man kindly.
"Well . . . about this much," said Millie and showed him her
purse. It was empty.
"I see . . ." muttered the man, and he looked up at the ceiling.
Millie looked up at the ceiling too. It was covered with
interesting patterns.

"Aha!" said the man suddenly. "I think I have just the thing for you, Madam. Wait here a moment, please."
And away he went to the back of the shop.
A few minutes later he returned with a box in his hands.
He placed it on a table and removed the lid.

"This is a most marvellous hat, Madam," said the man.
"It can be any size, shape or colour you wish. All you have to do is imagine it."

Carefully, the man took the hat out of the box and put it on Millie's head. It fitted her perfectly.

"Thank you," said Millie, "I like it very much!" She put her hand in her purse and handed the man all she had in it.

"Thank you, Madam," said the man. "Would you like your hat in its box?"

"No, thank you," said Millie, "I'll take it just as it is."

Millie felt happy in her new hat.
"But now I must think what my hat
is going to look like," she thought.
"Perhaps it has lots of feathers like
the one in the shop window,

only even more feathers . . ."

It was a peacock hat!

Millie stopped outside a cake shop
and looked in the window.
All the cakes looked delicious.

So Millie had a cake hat!

When Millie passed a flower shop
her hat became flowery . . .

. . . and in the park she wore a fountain hat!

Suddenly Millie saw that she was not the only one with a special hat . . .

Everyone had a hat of their own. And they were all different.

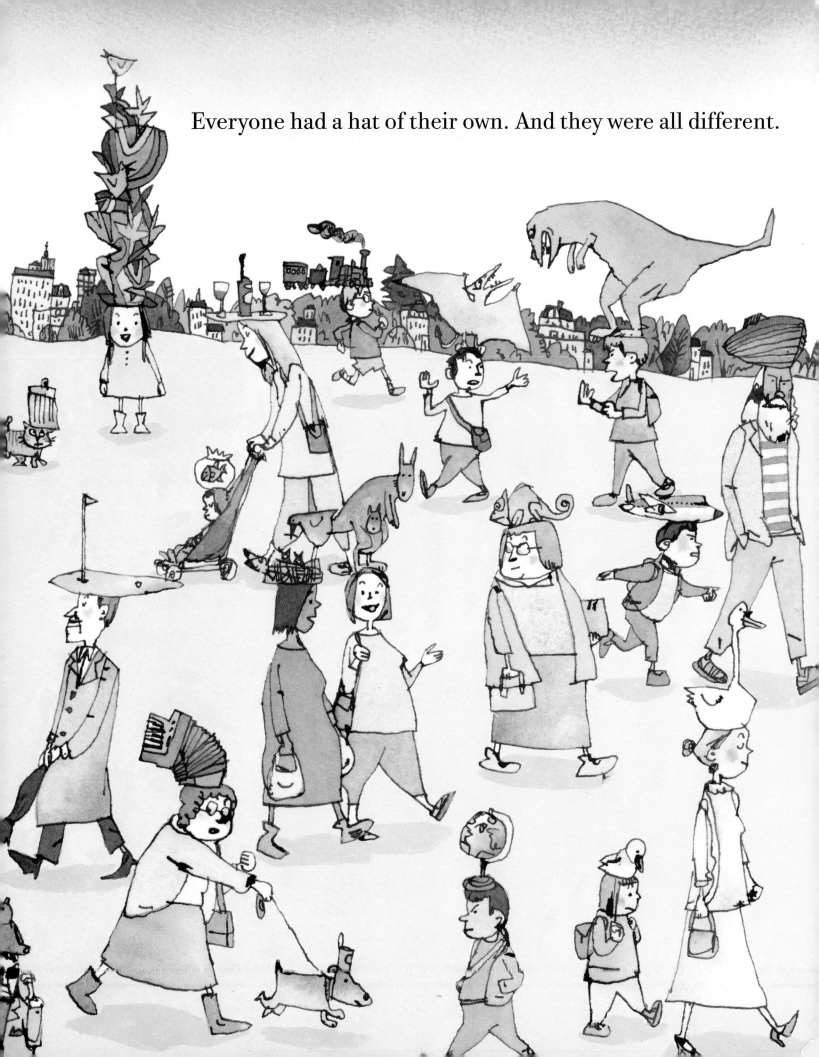

She saw an old lady
who was wearing a dark, murky pond hat.
Millie smiled at her and
the birds and the fish leapt out of
her hat and onto the old lady's.

Millie felt like singing.

And so did her hat.

By the time
Millie
arrived back
home, her
hat had
grown so
tall that
she
couldn't
walk
through
the door!

So she
thought of
another hat . . .

"How do you like my new hat?"
she asked when she saw her mum and dad.
"New hat?" said her mum. "But you haven't . . ."
Then she stopped and smiled. "It's a marvellous hat, Millie.
I wish I had one too."
"But you do have one," said Millie.
"You only have to imagine it!"

And she was right.
Everyone has their very own marvellous hat.